E-1

E
GAY

Gay, Michel

The Christmas wolf

MICHEL GAY

THE CHRISTMAS WOLF

GREENWILLOW BOOKS
New York

TO GRANDMOTHER MARINETTE

Copyright © 1980 by L'Ecole des Loisirs, Paris. Published in France under the title *Le Loup-Noël*.
All rights reserved. No part of this book may be reproduced or utilized in any form or by any means, electronic or mechanical, including photocopying, recording or by any information storage and retrieval system, without permission in writing from the Publisher, Greenwillow Books, a division of William Morrow & Co., Inc., 105 Madison Ave., New York, N.Y. 10016.   Printed in U.S.A.   First Edition
5 4 3 2 1

Library of Congress Cataloging in Publication Data
Gay, Michel.   The Christmas wolf.
Summary: When his children wonder why Father Christmas does not come to their mountain, Father Wolf goes to town to shop for Christmas presents with unforeseen results.
[1. Christmas—Fiction.   2. Wolves—Fiction]
I. Title.   PZ7.G238Ch 1983   [E]
83-1441   ISBN 0-688-02290-1
ISBN 0-688-02291-X (lib. bdg.)

The wolf family lived in an abandoned powerhouse, high in the mountains. From their home, they could see the entire valley. Colored lights twinkled in the town below. Christmas was coming.

"Why doesn't Father Christmas ever come to our mountain?"
asked the wolf children. Their parents didn't know what to say.

But Father Wolf
decided that something
must be done, and he left
for town. As he climbed to the
highway, he heard the sound of a motor.

He held up
his paw.
But instead of
stopping,
the truck
nearly hit him
and sped on.

Father Wolf barely managed to leap out of the way.

He landed in the town dump.

It gave him an idea.

He went back to the
highway and decided
to wait for a bus.

It picked him up and took
him into town. Nobody
paid any attention to him.

He saw a big store and headed for it—

right into a revolving door. He had never seen one before.

His boots, his cap, and his dark glasses flew off.

Inside the store, Father Wolf looked at everything.

"Make a lady happy—give her a jewel," urged a salesman.

"My wife would prefer a bone," said Father Wolf. "I mean a sweater."

"I have just the one," said a saleswoman. "It is made of camel's hair. You can feel how soft it is if you take off your gloves."

"It's lovely, but my wife prefers rabbit," said Father Wolf.

The salespeople stared. Father Wolf walked
toward a sign that said TOYS.

This is more like it, he thought. He was so excited
he forgot his disguise.

"Help, help! A wolf!" screamed a woman.
Everyone shouted and ran. A siren blared.

Police arrived quickly, but no one could find a wolf anywhere.

It was late that night before Father Wolf dared to move.

Sadly he started home.

It was a long way up the mountain, and he had
no presents to bring home.

Suddenly Father Wolf was blinded by headlights. The truck
drivers were returning from town. They had spotted him.

The truck came
straight at him
and skidded
when it hit him.

Father Wolf lay unconscious. The truck was balanced on the mountain's ledge. And the terrified drivers huddled inside.

After a time Father Wolf regained consciousness.
He was hurt, and he howled loudly.

Mother Wolf heard him.

And so did the truck drivers.
They were so frightened
they leaped out of the truck.
The truck tipped over and
hurtled down the mountain.
The men did not stop running
until they reached the town.

The next morning the wolf family was awakened by an excited squirrel.

"Come quickly," he called. "Father Christmas has come.
Father Christmas has come to our mountain."

EL CRYSTAL
MEDIA CENTER